P9-CDT-004

GOLDEN FAIRY TALE COLLECTION

ILLUSTRATED BY TONY WOLF
TEXT BY PETER HOLEINONE

First published in the United States 1990
by Gallery Books, an imprint of W. H. Smith Publishers, Inc.,
112 Madison Avenue, New York, New York 10016.

Gallery Books are available for bulk purchase for sales
promotions and premium use. For details write or telephone
the Manager of Special Sales, W. H. Smith Publishers, Inc.,
112 Madison Avenue, New York, New York 10016. (212) 532-6600

PRINTED BY
ARTI GRAFICHE MOTTA
MILANO - ITALY

The story of
PINOCCHIO
and other tales

GALLERY BOOKS
An Imprint of W. H. Smith Publishers Inc.
112 Madison Avenue
New York, New York 10016

Once upon a time . . .

. . . a carpenter, picked up a strange lump of wood one day while mending a table. When he began to chip it, the wood started to moan. This frightened the carpenter and he decided to get rid of it at once, so he gave it to a friend called Geppetto, who wanted to make a puppet. Geppetto, a cobbler, took his lump of wood home, thinking about the name he would give his puppet.

"I'll call him Pinocchio," he told himself. "It's a lucky name." Back in his humble basement home and workshop, Geppetto started to carve the wood. Suddenly a voice squealed:

"Ooh! That hurt!" Geppeto was astonished to find that the wood was alive. Excitedly he carved a head, hair and eyes, which immediately stared right at the cobbler. But the second Geppetto carved out the nose, it grew longer and longer, and no matter how often the cobbler cut it down to size, it just stayed a long nose. The newly cut mouth began to chuckle and when Geppetto angrily complained, the puppet stuck out his tongue at him. That was nothing, however! When the cobbler shaped the hands, they snatched the good man's wig, and the newly carved legs gave him a hearty kick. His eyes brimming with tears, Geppetto scolded the puppet.

"You naughty boy! I haven't even finished making you, yet you've no respect for your father!" Then he picked up the puppet and, a step at a time, taught him to walk. But the minute Pinocchio stood upright, he started to run about the room, with Geppetto after him, then he opened the door and dashed into the street. Now, Pinocchio ran faster than Geppetto and though the poor cobbler shouted "Stop him! Stop him!" none of the onlookers, watching in amusement, moved a finger. Luckily, a

policeman heard the cobbler's shouts and strode quickly down the street. Grabbing the runaway, he handed him over to his father.

"I'll box your ears," gasped Geppetto, still out of breath. Then he realised that was impossible, for in his haste to carve the puppet, he had forgotten to make his ears. Pinocchio had got a fright at being in the clutches of the police, so he apologised and Geppetto forgave his son.

Indeed, the minute they reached home, the cobbler made Pinocchio a suit out of flowered paper, a pair of bark shoes and a soft bread hat. The puppet hugged his father.

"I'd like to go to school," he said, "to become clever and help you when you're old!" Geppetto was touched by this kind thought.

"I'm very grateful," he replied, "but we haven't enough money even to buy you the first reading book!" Pinocchio looked downcast, then Geppetto suddenly rose to his feet, put on his old tweed coat and went out of the house. Not long after he returned carrying a first reader, but minus his coat. It was snowing outside.

"Where's your coat, father?"

"I sold it."

"Why did you sell it?"

"It kept me too warm!"

Pinocchio threw his arms round Geppetto's neck and kissed the kindly old man.

It had stopped snowing and Pinocchio set out for school with his first reading book under his arm. He was full of good intentions. "Today I want to learn to read. Tomorrow I'll learn to write and the day after to count. Then I'll earn some money and buy Geppetto a fine new coat. He deserves it, for . . ." The sudden sound of a brass band broke into the puppet's daydream and he soon forgot all about school. He ended up in a crowded square where people were clustering round a brightly coloured booth.

"What's that?" he asked a boy.

"Can't you read? It's the Great Puppet Show!"

"How much do you pay to go inside?"

"Fourpence."

"Who'll give me fourpence for this brand new book?" Pinocchio cried. A nearby junk seller bought the reading book and Pinocchio hurried into the booth. Poor Geppetto. His sacrifice had been quite in vain. Hardly had Pinocchio got inside, when he was seen by one of the puppets on the stage who cried out:

"There's Pinocchio! There's Pinocchio!"

"Come along. Come up here with us. Hurrah for brother Pinocchio!" cried the puppets. Pinocchio went onstage with his new friends, while the spectators below began to mutter about

the uproar. Then out strode Giovanni, the puppet-master, a frightful looking man with fierce bloodshot eyes.

"What's going on here? Stop that noise! Get in line, or you'll hear about it later!"

That evening, Giovanni sat down to his meal, but when he found that more wood was needed to finish cooking his nice chunk of meat, he remembered the intruder who had upset his show.

"Come here, Pinocchio! You'll make good firewood!" The poor puppet started to weep and plead.

"Save me, father! I don't want to die . . . I don't want to die!" When Giovanni heard Pinocchio's cries, he was surprised.

"Are your parents still alive?" he asked.

"My father is, but I've never known my mother," said the puppet in a low voice. The big man's heart melted.

"It would be beastly for your father if I did throw you into the fire . . . but I must finish roasting the mutton. I'll just have to burn another puppet. Men! Bring me Harlequin, trussed!" When Pinocchio saw that another puppet was going to be burned in his place, he wept harder than ever.

"Please don't, sir! Oh, sir, please don't! Don't burn Harlequin!"

"That's enough!" boomed Giovanni in a rage. "I want my meat well cooked!"

"In that case," cried Pinocchio defiantly, rising to his feet, "burn me! It's not right that Harlequin should be burnt instead of me!"

Giovanni was taken aback. "Well, well!" he said. "I've never met a puppet hero before!" Then he went on in a milder tone. "You really are a good lad. I might indeed . . ." Hope flooded Pinocchio's heart as the puppet-master stared at him, then at last the man said: "All right! I'll eat half-raw mutton tonight, but next time, somebody will find himself in a pickle." All the puppets were delighted at being saved. Giovanni asked Pinocchio to tell him the whole tale, and feeling sorry for kindhearted Geppetto, he gave the puppet five gold pieces.

"Take these to your father," he said. "Tell him to buy himself a new coat, and give him my regards."

Pinocchio cheerfully left the puppet booth after thanking Giovanni for being so generous. He was hurrying homewards when he met a half-blind cat and a lame fox. He couldn't help but tell them all about his good fortune, and when the pair set eyes on the gold coins, they hatched a plot, saying to Pinocchio:

"If you would really like to please your father, you ought to take him a lot more coins. Now, we know of a magic meadow where you can sow these five coins. The next day, you will find they have become ten times as many!"

"How can that happen?" asked Pinocchio in amazement.

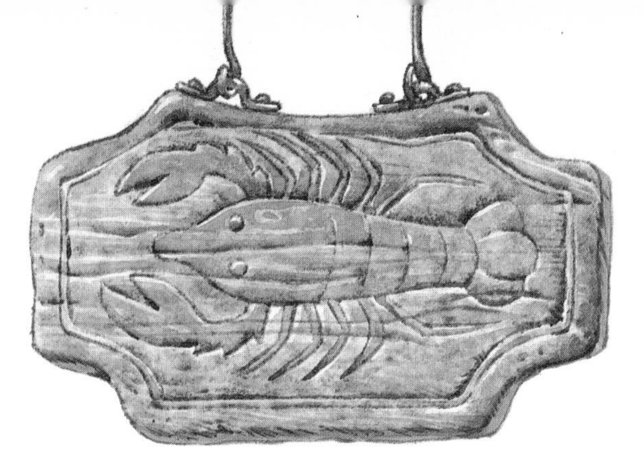

"I'll tell you how!" exclaimed the fox. "In the land of Owls lies a meadow known as Miracle Meadow. If you plant one gold coin in a little hole, next day you will find a whole tree dripping with gold coins!" Pinocchio drank in every word his two "friends" uttered and off they all went to the Red Shrimp Inn to drink to their meeting and future wealth.

After food and a short rest, they made plans to leave at midnight for Miracle Meadow. However, when Pinocchio was wakened by the innkeeper at the time arranged, he found that the fox and the cat had already left. All the puppet could do then was pay for the dinner, using one of his gold coins, and set off alone along the path through the woods to the magic meadow. Suddenly . . . "Your money or your life!" snarled two hooded bandits. Now, Pinocchio had hidden the coins under his tongue, so he could not say a word, and nothing the bandits could do would make Pinocchio tell where the coins were hidden. Still mute, even when the wicked pair tied a noose round the poor puppet's neck and pulled it tighter and tighter, Pinocchio's last thought was "Father, help me!"

Of course, the hooded bandits were the fox and the cat. "You'll hang there," they said, "till you decide to talk. We'll be back soon to see if you have changed your mind!" And away they went.

However, a fairy who lived nearby had overheard everything . . . From the castle window, the Turquoise Fairy saw a kicking puppet dangling from an oak tree in the wood. Taking pity on him, she clapped

her hands three times and suddenly a hawk and a dog appeared.

"Quickly!" said the fairy to the hawk. "Fly to that oak tree and with your beak snip away the rope round the poor lad's neck!"

To the dog she said: "Fetch the carriage and gently bring him to me!"

In no time at all, Pinocchio, looking quite dead, was lying in a cosy bed in the castle, while the fairy called three famous doctors, crow, owl and cricket. A very bitter medicine, prescribed by these three doctors quickly cured the puppet, then as she caressed him, the fairy said: "Tell me what happened!"

Pinocchio told her his story, leaving out the bit about selling his first reading book, but when the fairy asked him where the gold coins were, the puppet replied that he had lost them. In fact, they were hidden in one of his pockets. All at once, Pinocchio's nose began to stretch, while the fairy laughed.

"You've just told a lie! I know you have, because your nose is growing longer!" Blushing with shame, Pinocchio had no idea what to do with such an ungainly nose and he began to weep. However, again feeling sorry for him, the fairy clapped her hands and a flock of woodpeckers appeared to peck his nose back to its proper length.

"Now, don't tell any more lies," the fairy warned him, "or your nose will grow again! Go home and take these coins to your father."

Pinocchio gratefully hugged the fairy and ran off homewards. But near the oak tree in the forest, he bumped into the cat and the fox. Breaking his promise, he foolishly let himself be talked into burying the coins in the magic meadow. Full of hope, he returned next day, but the coins had gone. Pinocchio sadly trudged home without the coins Giovanni had given him for his father.

After scolding the puppet for his long absence, Geppetto forgave him and off he went to school. Pinocchio seemed to have calmed down a bit. But someone else was about to cross his path and lead him astray. This time, it was Carlo, the lazybones of the class.

"Why don't you come to Toyland with me?" he said. "Nobody ever studies there and you can play all day long!"

"Does such a place really exist?" asked Pinocchio in amazement.

"The wagon comes by this evening to take me there," said Carlo. "Would you like to come?"

Forgetting all his promises to his father and the fairy, Pinocchio was again heading for trouble. Midnight struck, and the wagon arrived to pick up the two friends, along with some other lads who could hardly wait to reach a place where schoolbooks and teachers had never been heard of. Twelve pairs of donkeys pulled the wagon, and they were all shod with white leather boots. The boys clambered into the wagon. Pinocchio, the most excited of them all, jumped on to a donkey. Toyland, here we come!

Now Toyland was just as Carlo had described it: the boys all had great fun and there were no lessons. You weren't even allowed to whisper the word "school", and Pinocchio could hardly believe he was able to play all the time.

"This is the life!" he said each time he met Carlo.

"I was right, wasn't I?" exclaimed his friend, pleased with himself.

"Oh, yes Carlo! Thanks to you I'm enjoying myself. And just think: teacher told me to keep well away from you."

One day, however, Pinocchio awoke to a nasty surprise. When he raised a hand to his head, he found he had sprouted a long pair of hairy ears, in place of the sketchy ears that Geppetto had never got round to finishing. And that wasn't all! The next day, they had grown longer than ever. Pinocchio shamefully pulled on a large cotton cap and went off to search for Carlo. He too was wearing a hat, pulled right down to his nose. With the same thought in their heads, the boys stared at each other, then snatching off their hats, they began to laugh at the funny sight of long hairy ears. But as they screamed with laughter, Carlo suddenly went pale and began to stagger. "Pinocchio, help! Help!" But Pinocchio himself was stumbling about and he burst into tears. For their faces were growing into the shape of a donkey's head and they felt themselves go down on all fours. Pinocchio and Carlo were turning into a pair of donkeys. And when they tried to groan with fear, they brayed loudly instead. When the Toyland wagon driver heard the braying of his new donkeys, he rubbed his hands in glee.

"There are two fine new donkeys to take to market. I'll get at least four gold pieces for them!" For such was the awful fate that awaited naughty little boys that played truant from school to spend all their time playing games.

Carlo was sold to a farmer, and a circus man bought Pinocchio to teach him to do tricks like his other performing animals. It was a hard life for a donkey! Nothing to eat but hay, and when that was gone, nothing but straw. And the beatings! Pinocchio was beaten every day till he had mastered the difficult circus tricks. One day, as he was jumping through the hoop, he stumbled and went lame. The circus man called the stable boy.

"A lame donkey is no use to me," he said. "Take it to market and get rid of it at any price!" But nobody wanted to buy a useless donkey. Then along came a little man who said: "I'll take

it for the skin. It will make a good drum for the village band!"

And so, for a few pennies, Pinocchio changed hands and he brayed sorrowfully when he heard what his awful fate was to be. The puppet's new owner led him to the edge of the sea, tied a large stone to his neck, and a long rope round Pinocchio's legs and pushed him into the water. Clutching the end of the rope, the man sat down to wait for Pinocchio to drown. Then he would flay off the donkey's skin.

Pinocchio struggled for breath at the bottom of the sea, and in a flash, remembered all the bother he had given Geppetto, his broken promises too, and he called on the fairy.

The fairy heard Pinocchio's call and when she saw he was about to drown, she sent a shoal of big fish. They ate away all the donkey flesh, leaving the wooden Pinocchio. Just then, as the fish stopped nibbling, Pinocchio felt himself hauled out of the water. And the man gaped in astonishment at the living puppet, twisting and turning like an eel, which appeared in place of the dead donkey. When he recovered his wits, he babbled, almost in tears: "Where's the donkey I threw into the sea?"

"I'm that donkey," giggled Pinocchio.

"You!" gasped the man. "Don't try pulling my leg. If I get angry . . ."

However, Pinocchio told the man the whole story . . . "and that's how you come to have a live puppet on the end of the rope instead of a dead donkey!"

"I don't give a whit for your story," shouted the man in a rage. "All I know is that I paid twenty coins for you and I want my money back! Since there's no donkey, I'll take *you* to market and sell you as firewood!"

By then free of the rope, Pinocchio made a face at the man and dived into the sea. Thankful to be a wooden puppet again, Pinocchio swam happily out to sea and was soon just a dot on the horizon. But his adventures were far from over. Out of the water behind him loomed a terrible giant shark! A horrified Pinocchio saw its wide open jaws and tried to swim away as fast as he could, but the monster only glided closer. Then the puppet tried to escape by going in the other direction, but in vain. He could never escape the shark, for as the water rushed into its cavern-like mouth, he was sucked in with it. And in an instant Pinocchio had been swallowed along with shoals of fish unlucky enough to be in the fierce creature's path. Down he went, tossed in the torrent of water as it poured down the shark's throat, till he felt dizzy. When Pinocchio came to his senses, he was in darkness. Over his head, he could hear the loud heave of the shark's gills. On his hands and knees, the puppet crept down what felt like a sloping path, crying as he went:

"Help! Help! Won't anybody save me?"

Suddenly, he noticed a pale light and, as he crept towards it, he saw it was a flame in the distance. On he went, till: "Father! It can't be you! . . ."

"Pinocchio! Son! It really is you . . ."

Weeping for joy, they hugged each other and, between sobs, told their adventures. Geppetto stroked the puppet's head and told him how he came to be in the shark's stomach.

"I was looking for you everywhere. When I couldn't find you on dry land, I made a boat to search for you on the sea. But the boat capsized in a storm, then the shark gulped me down. Luckily, it also swallowed bits of ships wrecked in the tempest, so I've managed to survive by getting what I could from these!"

"Well, we're still alive!" remarked Pinocchio, when they had finished recounting their adventures. "We must get out of here!" Taking Geppetto's hand, the pair started to climb up the shark's stomach, using a candle to light their way. When they got as far as its jaws, they took fright, but as it so happened, this shark slept with its mouth open, for it suffered from asthma.

"Now's our chance to escape," whispered Pinocchio. In a second he was in the water, swimming as quickly as he could, with Geppetto on his back.

As luck would have it, the shark had been basking in shallow waters since the day before, and Pinocchio soon reached the beach. Dawn was just breaking, and Geppetto, soaked to the skin, was half dead with cold and fright.

"Lean on me, father." said Pinocchio. "I don't know where we are, but we'll soon find our way home!"

Beside the sands stood an old hut made of branches, and there they took shelter. Geppetto was running a temperature, but Pinocchio went out, saying, “I’m going to get you some milk.” The bleating of goats led the puppet in the right direction, and he soon came upon a farmer. Of course, he had no money to pay for the milk.

“My donkey’s dead,” said the farmer. “If you work the treadmill from dawn to noon, then you can have some milk.” And so, for days on end, Pinocchio rose early each morning to earn Geppetto’s food.

At long last, Pinocchio and Geppetto reached home. The puppet worked late into the night weaving reed baskets to make money for his father and himself. One day, he heard that the fairy after a wave of bad luck, was ill in hospital. So instead of buying himself a new suit of clothes, Pinocchio sent the fairy the money to pay for her treatment.

One night, in a wonderful dream, the fairy appeared to reward Pinocchio for his kindness. When the puppet looked in the mirror next morning, he found he had turned into somebody else. For there in the mirror, was a handsome young lad with blue eyes and brown hair. Geppetto hugged him happily.

“Where’s the old wooden Pinocchio?” the young lad asked in astonishment.

“There!” exclaimed Geppetto, pointing at him. “When bad boys become good, their looks change along with their lives!”

WHAT OTHER PEOPLE THINK

Once upon a time . . . a farmer and his son went to market to sell a donkey. However, they loaded the beast into the wheelbarrow, so that it would not reach market tired and worn out, and pushed it along the road. When people saw such a peculiar sight, they loudly remarked: "That man is mad! Whoever saw a donkey being taken to market in a wheelbarrow!"

The poor farmer became more and more confused, for the farther he went, the louder the comments became and the more people gossiped. It was the last straw when, as they passed the blacksmith's forge, the smith jeeringly asked the farmer if he wanted shoeing, since he was doing the donkey work! So the farmer stopped, heaved the animal out of the wheelbarrow and climbed onto its back, while his son walked behind.

But that made matters even worse!

A group of women going home from market instantly complained: "You cruel man! Fancy a great lump like you riding a donkey, while your poor little boy runs along behind! You ought to be ashamed of yourself!"

People heaped insult upon insult, till the unhappy farmer slid off the donkey. He simply did not know what to do next. He took off his cap and mopped his brow.

"Whew!" he exclaimed. "I never imagined it could be so difficult to take a donkey to market."

Then he hoisted his little boy onto the donkey and walked along behind. This time, a cluster of men began to protest.

"Look at that! There's a young lad sitting pretty as you please on top of a donkey, while his weary old father has to go on foot!"

"It's a disgrace."

Once again, father and son came to a halt. How on earth could they stop people from criticizing everything they did? Well, in the end, they *both* got on the donkey.

"What heartless folk!" exclaimed the passers-by. "Two riders on one little donkey!" But by now the farmer had lost his patience. He gave the donkey a terrible kick, saying:

"Giddy up! From now on, I'll do things my way, and pay no attention to what other people think!"

CHICO AND THE CRANE

Once upon a time . . . in the city of Florence lived Mr Corrado, a nobleman famous for his love of hunting and for his banquets. One day, his falcon caught a beautiful crane, which Mr Corrado handed to the cook and told him to roast to perfection.

The bird was almost done when a pretty young peasant girl entered the kitchen to visit the cook. When she sniffed the savoury smell of roasting, the girl persuaded Chico to give her one of the bird's legs. In due course, the crane was carried to the nobleman's table and Mr Corrado summoned the cook to explain what had happed to the missing leg. To his question, the unfortunate cook replied:

"Sire! Cranes have only one leg!"

"What? One leg?" exclaimed Mr Corrado. "Do you think I've never seen a crane before?" But Chico insisted that these birds had only one leg: "If I had a live bird here, I'd show you!" However, the nobleman had no desire to argue in front of his guests, but he told the cook:

"Very well. We'll go and see tomorrow morning, but woe betide you if it's not true."

At sunrise, Mr Corrado, angrier than ever, gave the order to saddle the horses. "Now we'll see who's telling lies," he said grimly. Chico would gladly have fled in fear, but he did not dare. However, as they approached the river, the cook spotted a flock of cranes, fast asleep. Of course, they were all standing on one leg, as they do when resting. "Sire! Sire!" Chico cried. "Look, I was right. They have only one leg."

"Indeed!" snorted Mr Corrado. "I'll show you!" And so saying, he clapped his hands and gave a shout. At the sudden sound, the cranes uncurled the other leg and flapped away.

"There you are, you scoundrel," growled the nobleman. "You see they have two legs!" To which Chico quickly retorted, "But Sire, if you had clapped and shouted at table yesterday, then the bird would have uncurled its other leg!"

At such a clever reply, Mr Corrado's anger turned to amusement. "Yes, Chico, you're right. I should have done just that!" And he clapped the cook's shoulder, as they parted friends.

THE THREE WISHES

Once upon a time . . . a woodcutter lived happily with his wife in a pretty little log cabin in the middle of a thick forest. Each morning he set off singing to work, and when he came home in the evening, a plate of hot steaming soup was always waiting for him.

One day, however, he had a strange surprise. He came upon a big fir tree with strange open holes on the trunk. It looked somehow different from the other trees, and just as he was about to chop it down, the alarmed face of an elf popped out of a hole.

"What's all this banging?" asked the elf. "You're not thinking of cutting down this tree, are you? It's my home. I live here!" The

woodcutter dropped his axe in astonishment.

"Well, I . . ." he stammered.

"With all the other trees there are in this forest, you have to pick this one. Lucky I was in, or I would have found myself homeless."

Taken aback at these words, the woodcutter quickly recovered, for after all the elf was quite tiny, while he himself was a big hefty chap, and he boldly replied: "I'll cut down any tree I like, so . . ."

"All right! All right!" broke in the elf. "Shall we put it this way: if you don't cut down *this* tree, I grant you three wishes. Agreed?" The woodcutter scratched his head.

"Three wishes, you say? Yes, I agree." And he began to hack at another tree. As he worked and sweated at his task, the woodcutter kept thinking about the magic wishes.

"I'll see what my wife thinks . . ."

The woodcutter's wife was busily cleaning a pot outside the house when her husband arrived. Grabbing her round the waist, he twirled her in delight.

"Hooray! Hooray! Our luck is in!"

The woman could not understand why her husband was so pleased with himself and she shrugged herself free. Later, however, over a glass of fine wine at the table, the woodcutter told his wife of his meeting with the elf, and she too began to picture the wonderful things that the elf's three wishes might give them. The woodcutter's wife took a first sip of wine from her husband's glass.

"Nice," she said, smacking her lips. "I wish I had a string of sausages to go with it, though . . ."

Instantly she bit her tongue, but too late. Out of the air appeared the sausages, while the woodcutter stuttered with rage.

". . . what have you done! Sausages . . . What a stupid waste of a wish! You foolish woman. I wish they would stick up your nose!" No sooner said than done. For the sausages leapt up and stuck fast to the end of the woman's nose. This time, the woodcutter's wife flew into a rage.

"You idiot, what have *you* done? With all the things we could have wished for . . ." The mortified woodcutter, who had just repeated his wife's own mistake, exclaimed:

"I'd chop . . ." Luckily he stopped himself in time, realising with horror that he'd been on the point of having his tongue chopped off. As his wife complained and blamed him, the poor man burst out laughing.

"If only you knew how funny you look with those sausages on the end of your nose!" Now that really upset the woodcutter's wife. She hadn't thought of her looks. She tried to tug away the sausages but they would not budge. She pulled again and again, but in vain. The sausages were firmly attached to her nose. Terrified, she exclaimed: "They'll be there for the rest of my life!"

Feeling sorry for his wife and wondering how he could ever put up with a woman with such an awkward nose, the woodcutter said: "I'll try."

Grasping the string of sausages, he tugged with all his might. But he simply pulled his wife over on top of him. The pair sat on the floor, gazing sadly at each other.

"What shall we do now?" they said, each thinking the same thought.

"There's only one thing we *can* do . . ." ventured the woodcutter's wife timidly.

"Yes, I'm afraid so . . ." her husband sighed, remembering their dreams of riches, and he bravely wished the third and last wish: "I wish the sausages would leave my wife's nose."

And they did. Instantly, husband and wife hugged each other tearfully, saying: "Maybe we'll be poor, but we'll be happy again!"

That evening, the only reminder of the woodcutter's meeting with the elf was the string of sausages. So the couple fried them, gloomily thinking of what that meal had cost them.

ALI AND THE SULTAN'S SADDLE

Once upon a time . . . there lived a very powerful Sultan whose kingdom stretched to the edges of the desert. One of his subjects was called Ali, a man who enjoyed making fun of his ruler. He invented all sorts of tales about the Sultan and his Court, and folk would roar with laughter at his jokes. Indeed, Ali became so well known, that people pointed him out in the street and chuckled.

Ali's fun at the Sultan's expense reached the point where the Sultan himself heard about it. Angry and insulted, he ordered the guards to bring the joker before him.

"I shall punish him for his cheek," said the Sultan eagerly, as he rubbed his hands, thinking of the good whipping he was about to administer.

But when Ali was brought before him, he bowed so low that his forehead scraped the floor. Giving the Sultan no time to open his mouth, Ali said:

"Sire! Please let me thank you for granting my dearest wish: to look upon you in person and tell you how greatly I admire your wisdom and handsome figure. I've written a poem about you. May I recite it to you?"

Overwhelmed by this stream of words and delighted at Ali's unexpected praise, the Sultan told him to recite his poem. In actual fact, Ali hadn't written a single word, so he had to invent it as he went along, and this he did, loudly comparing the Sultan's splendour to that of the sun, his strength to that of the tempest and his voice to the sound of the wind. Everyone applauded and cheered. Now quite charmed, the Sultan forgot why he had called Ali before him, and clapped at the end of the poem in his honour.

"Well done!" he cried. "You're a fine poet and deserve a reward. Choose one of these saddles as payment for your ability." Ali picked up a donkey's saddle and, thanking the Sultan, he hurried out of the palace with the saddle on his back. When people saw him rush along, they all asked him:

"Ali, where are you going with that donkey's saddle on your back?"

"I've just recited a poem in honour of the Sultan, and he's given me one of his own robes as a reward!"

And winking, Ali pointed to the saddle!

AMIN AND THE EGGS

Once upon a time . . . a peasant called Amin lost all his crops from his miserable little plot in a drought. He decided to seek his fortune in another village, and off he went on his donkey. On credit, he obtained a dozen hard-boiled eggs from a merchant for his journey.

Seven years later, Amin returned to his village. This time he was riding a fine black horse, followed by a servant on a camel laden with gold and silver coins. Amin had become a rich man and the news of this soon spread through the village. Straight away, the merchant who had given him the dozen eggs on credit knocked at Amin's door, asking for five hundred silver pieces in payment of the old debt. Amin of course refused to pay such a large sum and the matter was taken before the judge.

On the day of the hearing, the merchant appeared in court at the appointed time, but of Amin there was no sign. The judge waited impatiently for a quarter of an hour, and was on the point of adjourning the hearing, when Amin dashed in, out of breath. At once, the merchant said, in defence of his demands:

"I asked Amin for payment of five hundred silver coins, because twelve chickens might have hatched from the eggs he bought from me on credit, seven years ago. These chickens

would have become hens and cockerels; more eggs would have been laid, these too would have hatched, and so on. After seven years, I might have had a great flock of fowls!"

"Of course," agreed the judge. "Perfectly right." And turning to Amin with a hostile air, he ordered: "What have you to say for yourself? And, by the way, why are you late?" Amin did not turn a hair.

"I had a plate of boiled beans in the house and I planted them in the garden to have a good crop next year!"

"Fool!" exclaimed the judge. "Since when do boiled beans grow?" To which Amin promptly retorted:

"And since when do boiled eggs hatch into chickens?"

He had won his case.

SALEM AND THE NAIL

Once upon a time . . . the shop belonging to an astute merchant called Salem, and all the carpets in it, were burnt in a fire. Salem was left with nothing but his house, and since he was a trader he decided to sell it. With the money he would be able to buy a new shop and more carpets. Salem did not ask a high price for his house. However, he had a most unusual request to make of would-be buyers: "I'll sell you the house, except for that nail in the wall. That remains mine!" And as they all went off, shaking their heads, they wondered what he meant by this strange remark.

Abraham, however, more miserly than all the others, thought the price was fair, and he even haggled it down further. A bargain was struck and the new owner took over the whole house, except for the nail. A week later, Salem knocked at the door.

"I've come to hang something on my nail," he said. Abraham let him in and Salem hung up a large empty bag, said goodbye and left. A few days later, he appeared again, and this time hung an old cloak on the nail. From then on, Salem's visits became regular; he was forever coming and going, taking things off the nail or hanging something else up.

One evening, in front of the stunned eyes of Abraham and his family, Salem arrived dragging a dead donkey. With a struggle, he hoisted it up and roped it to the nail. The occupants of the house complained about the smell and the sight of the dead beast, but Salem calmly said: "It's my nail and I can hang anything I like on it!"

Abraham, naturally, could no longer live in the house under such conditions. But Salem refused to remove the donkey.

"If you don't like it," he said, "you can get out of my house, but I'll not pay you back a penny!"

Abraham did his best to persuade Salem to take the donkey down, for it smelt to high heaven. He even consulted a judge, but the terms of the bargain were clear. The house belonged to Abraham, but Salem kept the nail.

In the end, Abraham was forced to leave, and Salem got his house back without paying a penny for it!

THE GOLDEN GOOSE

Once upon a time . . . there was a woodcutter called Thaddeus, a dreamy, foolish-looking lad though good-hearted. One day, his father sent him to a distant wood to chop down trees. Thaddeus thought that these trees were a kind he had never seen before and that it was hard work trying to hack through their hard trunks. Sweating after all his efforts, he had barely sat down against a sawn-off trunk to have a meal, when a strange old man with a white beard popped out from behind a bush and asked him for a bite to eat. Kindly Thaddeus gave him some bread and cheese and together they cheerily drank a flask of wine.

"Of all the woodcutters that have tried to fell these trees, you're the first one who has been nice to me," said the old man, stuttering, perhaps after all the wine. "You deserve a reward. If you cut down that tree in the centre of the wood, you'll find that all the others will fall down by themselves. Have a look in its roots where there's a gift for you! You see, I'm the Wizard of the Woods!"

Not particularly surprised, Thaddeus did as he was told, and in a flash, his work was done. From the roots of the tree the Wizard had pointed towards, the woodcutter took a golden goose. Slipping the bird under his arm, Thaddeus set off homewards. Now, it may have been too much wine, or maybe the fact he was new to these parts, but the fact remains that Thaddeus lost his way. At dead of night, he reached a strange village. A tavern was still open, so the woodcutter went in.

"Something to eat for myself and for the Golden Goose that the Wizard of the Woods gave me," he ordered the innkeeper's daughter. "That's a bite for me and a bite for you," he said, sharing his food with the goose across the table. The innkeeper's other two daughters came to stare at the strange sight, then all three dared ask: "Why are you so kind to a goose?"

"This is a magic goose," replied Thaddeus, "and worth a fortune. I shall stay the night here and I need a secure room, for I don't want to be robbed."

However, during the night, one of the sisters was persuaded to steal at least one goose feather.

"If it's a magic bird, then one of its feathers will be precious too!" But the second her hand touched the goose's tail, it stuck fast, and nothing would unstick it. In a low voice, she called her sisters, but when they tried to pull her free, they too stuck fast. A little later, Thaddeus woke, not at all surprised to see the three sisters, ashamed at being discovered, stuck to the golden goose.

"How can we get free?" they wailed. But the woodcutter coolly replied:

"I have to leave with my goose. Too bad for you if you're stuck to her. You'll just have to come too!" And when the innkeeper saw the strange little procession trip past, he shouted "What's up?" and grabbed the last sister by the arm. It was the worst thing he could have done! For he too found himself attached to the tail of the little group. The same fate awaited a nosy village woman, the plump curate and the baker who had placed a hand on the curate's shoulder as he rushed past. Last of all came a guard who had tried to stop the procession. People laughed as Thaddeus and his row of followers went by, and crowds soon flocked the roads.

Close to the village where Thaddeus had spent the night stood the Royal Palace. Though rich and powerful, the King had a great sorrow: his only daughter suffered from a strange illness that no doctor had been able to cure. She was always sad and unhappy. The King had once proclaimed that the man who succeeded in making his daughter laugh would be granted her hand in marriage. But so far, nobody had so much as brought a smile to the Princess's lips.

As it so happened, the Princess chose that day to drive through the village square, just as the woodcutter with the goose under his arm, solemnly marched by with his line of unwilling followers. When she heard the people chuckle, the Princess raised the carriage curtains. The minute she set eyes on the amazing sight, she burst into peals of laughter.

Everyone was amazed to hear the Princess laugh for the first time. She stepped down from the carriage for a closer look at the golden goose and that's how she got stuck to the baker! Laughing and chattering, the procession headed towards the palace, with the crowds at their heels. When the King saw his daughter in fits of laughter, he could hardly believe it.

"How amazing! How amazing!" he said.

But in spite of all the mirth, it was a serious situation. That is, until a large man with a tall peaked hat and a white beard stepped forward and snapped his fingers three times. Suddenly, Thaddeus and the others all became unstuck. The woodcutter was about to thank the Wizard of the Woods, for it could be none other, but he had vanished into thin air. And that's how the simple woodcutter, Thaddeus, found himself married to the King's daughter.

THE MUSICIANS OF BREMEN

Once upon a time . . . an old donkey was ill-treated by his master. Tired of such unkindness, he decided to run away, and when he heard that Bremen was looking for singers with the town band, he decided that someone with a fine braying voice like his might be accepted.

As he went along the road, the donkey met a skinny dog, covered with sores.

"Come with me. If you have a good bark, you'll find a job with the band too. Just wait and see!"

A little later, a stray cat, no longer able to catch mice, joined them and the trio trotted hopefully on towards the town. As they passed a farmyard, they stopped to admire an elderly cockerel who, with outstretched wings, was crowing to the skies.

"You sing well," they told him. "What are you so happy about?"

"Happy?" muttered the cockerel with tears in his eyes. "They want to put me in the pot and make broth of me. I'm singing as hard as I can today, for tomorrow I'll be gone." But the donkey told him, "Run away with us. With a voice like yours, you'll be famous in Bremen!"

Now there were four of them. The way was long, night fell, and very frightened, the four creatures found themselves in a thick forest.

They scarcely knew whether to press on or to hide in some caves and rest. Suddenly, in the distance they saw a light amongst the trees. It came from a little cottage and they crept up to the window. The donkey placed his front hoofs on the window ledge. Anxious to see, the dog jumped on the donkey's back, the cat climbed onto the dog and the cockerel flew on top of the cat to watch what was going on inside.

Now, the cottage was the hideaway of a gang of bandits who were busily celebrating their latest robbery. The hungry donkey and his friends became excited when they saw the food on the table. Upset by

the jittery crew on his back, the donkey stuck his head through the window and toppled his three companions on to the lamp. The light went out and the room rang with the braying of the donkey who had cut his nose on the glass, the barking of the dog and the snarling of the cat. The cockerel screeched along with the others.

Taken completely by surprise, the terrified bandits fled screaming: “The Devil! The Devil!” And their abandoned meal ended up in the four friends’ stomachs.

Later, however, just as the donkey and his companions were dropping off to sleep, one of the bandits crept back to the now quiet house and went in to find out what had taken place. He opened the door, and with his pistol in his hand, he stepped trembling towards the fire. However, mistaking the glow of the cat's eyes for burning coals, he thrust a candle between them and instantly the furious cat sank its claws into the bandit's face. The man fell backwards on to the dog, dropping his gun, which went off, and the animal's sharp teeth sank into his leg. When the donkey saw the bandit's figure at the door, he gave a tremendous kick, sending the man flying right through the doorway. The cockerel greeted this feat with a grim crowing sound.

"Run!" screamed the bandit. "Run! A horrible witch in there scratched my face, a demon bit me on the leg and a monster beat me with a stick! And . . ." But the other bandits were no longer listening, for they had taken to their heels and fled.

And so the donkey, the dog, the cat and the cockerel took over the house without any trouble and, with the booty left behind by the bandits, always had food on the table, and lived happy and contented for many years.